Disney
WRECK-IT RALPH

Sugar Rush Race!

By Billy Wrecks
Illustrated by the Disney Storybook Artists

Random House 🏠 New York

ISBN: 978-0-7364-2961-0
randomhouse.com/kids
MANUFACTURED IN CHINA
10 9 8 7 6 5 4 3 2 1

3-D special effects and production: Red Bird Publishing Ltd., U.K.

Wreck-It Ralph was a video game Bad Guy. Whenever someone played *Fix-It Felix Jr.*, it was his job to yell, "I'm gonna wreck it!" Then he would smash the Niceland apartment building floor by floor!

Fix-It Felix, the game's Good Guy, would then fix everything.
The Nicelanders, who lived in the building, would give Felix pies
and a medal. Then they would throw poor Ralph

off the roof
and into
a puddle
of mud.

One day, Ralph decided to sneak into a game called *Hero's Duty* and win a medal. Once he had a medal, Ralph thought, the Nicelanders would have to treat him like a Good Guy for a change.

Unfortunately, *Hero's Duty* was scary. It was filled with monstrous cy-bugs. And one of the soldiers in the game, Sergeant Calhoun, kept yelling at Ralph. He grabbed a medal and got out fast!

But Ralph ended up in another game world—one made entirely of sweets.

"*Sugar Rush*? Oh, no!" Ralph moaned. "This is that candy go-kart game." And to make matters worse, his medal was up in the branches of a peppermint tree.

A girl named Vanellope von Schweetz thought the medal was a coin she could use to enter the Sugar Rush races.

Vanellope grabbed the medal and ran to enter a big race against all the go-kart drivers in *Sugar Rush*.

"Yes!" Vanellope cheered when the medal was accepted as a coin. "I'm in!"

The only problem was that no one else in *Sugar Rush* wanted
her to race—especially King Candy. And the other racers were
mean to Vanellope. They called her names and wrecked her kart.
They even threw her in the mud!

Vanellope told Ralph she would get the medal back if she won the race. She promised to return the medal to him if he would help her. So they sneaked into the kart bakery and baked a new kart. Vanellope loved it. "It's perfect!" she cried.

Vanellope turned out to be a natural racer. She passed all the karts on the track until only King Candy was in front of her. He tried every dirty trick he knew to stop her.

Vanellope easily took the lead! But just as she was about to win, the finish line was destroyed by the cy-bugs from *Hero's Duty*!

Luckily, Ralph was able to get help from Fix-It Felix and Sergeant Calhoun. In no time, the finish line was fixed, and Vanellope rolled across it. She was a real racer at last!

"You belong in *Sugar Rush*," Ralph told Vanellope. Everyone in *Sugar Rush* cheered and told her that they were sorry for the way they had treated her.

By helping Vanellope, Ralph realized that being a Bad Guy was only his job. Deep down, he was really a good guy—and he didn't need a medal to prove it.